Sunlight point
Sonnenlichtpunkt

Marion Wolters

Dancable texts

General information
Perls are more than 1000 years old
in colours which are warm and cold.
As a means of payment and exchange
they are status symbols with a high range.
You can receive for them gold, spices and silk,
rather than bread, butter and milk.

Used until the 16th century in the Middle East
they were worn at rites of initiation and wedding feasts.
As an investment which was save,
as a present for people who were well-behaved.
With cobalt you can create true blue,
copper gives green a clue.
Manganese helps purple to be created,
iron assists yellow to be generated.
It is iron oxide that makes pearls brown,
the roots of a tree, but not its crown.

Glasblowers
Glass, Germanic 'Glas'
is a special class.
Shiny, gleaming, amber,
like the famous chamber.

Forest glassworks which were burning a lot of wood
could help
to melt

quite a lot of glass,
otherwise wood transport would be a farce.

Created between 1900 and 1950
Pigeon Egg Beads are translucent and nifty.
In Bohemia wedding pearls were found in triangular and
drop shape,
you can watch their manifold forms in many tapes.
Colourful, single coloured, with lines and cebra stripes
they were an asset for many hypes.
Germany's Rocaille beads are bulled in glass tubes by hand
with a tinier diameter known both by sea and by land.

Wadi Natrun
Wadi Natrun is the gate
for sodium carbonate.
For glass production
as an action
1450 before the computation of time
next to the desert with salt rime
is Thebes or Luxor
as it was named before.

Venice/Murano
Millefiori (thousand flowers)
were not ours
100 years ago
with a profile that was low
they were transported to Africa
where they became a star.

The fear of the glass furnices' fire and town's destruction
triggered the fear that the art's secret of beads'
production
was let out.
'It is our pride' they shout.

They were outsourced to the Isle of Murano
1295 was the anno.
In 1500 the Venetians invented beads
which leads
to a 12 point star moulds in blue-white-red
it could be found on rich people's heads.

Glass discolouration by manganese oxide
hide the hard work it took to imitate Chinese porcelain
milk glass was the solution for every woman and man.

Meriam puts down the texts. She is content with her first
text drafts which she will put the finishing touches to in
the course of the afternoon.

Tanzbare Texte

Allgemeine Informationen
Als Wertanlage und Statussymbol
sind Handelsperlen von innen hohl.
Sexy Gestalt

mit Gehalt,
mehr als 1000 Jahre alt.

Sie können sie gebrauchen, sich an ihnen berauschen.
Sie können für sie viel Geld zahlen oder sie tauschen,
gegen Seide, Gewürze und Gold,
sei der Handelsgott Ihnen hold!

Getragen nicht nur bei Riten der Initiation
und schon
sind Sie bereit sie zu tragen für die Zeit zu zweit
bei der Hochzeit.

Bis zum 16. Jahrhundert nur im Vorderen Orient und
Mittelmeerraum,
danach waren Handelsperlen auch für Westafrika ein
Traum.

Mit Kobalt erzeugt man blau,
schöne Perlen für Mann und Frau.
Grün wird Glas durch Kupfer,
ein willkommener Farbtupfer.
Violett färbt es sich durch Mangan,
so mancher Käufer war angetan.
Worauf könnte gelb verweisen?
Auf Eisen!
Seine braune Farbe entsteht durch Eisenoxid -
singen wir ein erdfarbenes Glaslied!

Glasbläser
„Glaza", germanisch Glas
bedeutet das:
glänzend, schimmernd, Bernstein sein.

So viel Holz für die Öfen zum Schmelzen,
da kann es helfen,
die Glashütten im Wald zu bauen,
sich den Elfen anzuvertrauen.

Pigeon Egg Beads sind durchscheinend,
wohlmeinend hergestellt von 1900-1950
sind sie nicht günstig.

Perlen in Tropfen- oder in Dreiecksform
sind in Böhmen für Hochzeiten die Norm.
Enorm mit nur einer Farbe, Linien, Zebrastreifen
kann man mit ihnen Melodien pfeifen.

Rocaille-Perlen mit winzigem Durchmesser
sind ein guter Gradmesser
für winzige Glasröhrchen gezogen von Hand,
sind sie nicht nur in Deutschland bekannt.

Wadi Natrun
Glasschmuck für Pharaonen,
die thronen.
Vor mehr als 1000 Jahre vor unserer Zeit
war es soweit:
in Mesopotamien und Luxor, früher Theben,
ließ man kunsthandwerklich die Erde beben

mit Handelsperlen, die Aufsehen erregen.
Im Wadi Natrun war das Natron aus den Seen ein Segen,
um mit Exporten und in Alexandria die Wirtschaft zu
beleben.

Venedig/Murano
Die Chevronperle wurde von den Venezianern erfunden.
Sie sollten sie unbedingt heute erkunden.
Zwölfzackig, mit sternförmiger Musterung blau-weiß-rot
lag sie schon ab 1500 mit im Überseeboot.

Handelsperlen namens Millefiore (1000 Blumen)
reisten in hohem Volumen
vor mehr als 100 Jahren -
wir sollten sie gut bewahren -
auf dem Handelsweg nach Afrika,
nur wenige sind noch immer da.

Im 16. Jahrhundert wurden in Venedig die Glasmacher
wach
und ahmten chinesisches Porzellan nach.
Milchglas, lattimo, von Milch italienisch „latte",
die Farbgebung ähnlich, doch schöner als Watte.

Wer setzt schon gern die Stadt mit Glasöfen in Brand?
Sie wurden von Venedig auf Murano verbannt.
Der Verrat der Perlenerzeugungskunst verhunzt die
Gewinne.

So wurde das Ersinnen, die Insel zu verlassen
auf Lebenszeit nicht zugelassen.

Glasentfärbung durch Manganoxid
gab es noch nicht zu den Zeiten von Ovid.
Erst auf Murano entstand der Christallo,
erzeugte in der Welt ein großes Hallo.

Meriam legt die Texte weg. Sie ist zufrieden mit ihren
ersten Textentwürfen, denen sie im Laufe des Nachmittags
den letzten Schliff geben wird.

The transparent lightness of sensitivity

After the preliminary discussion for an official event, the copywriter Meriam was invited as a duo singer. It was a day on which her professional role allowed her to be herself. She wore her old, shaggy, black favourite pullover and had already rehearsed with the band before.

She was not prepared for the force of their encounter. She had the feeling that she wanted to have children with him. She was lucky that their encounter happened nearly hidden from the world. Those who realized it remained silent.

He was not a slow man. He had thought through his decisions in advance, which seemed to be quickly and accurate.

His clothes were inconspicuously, they did not show his position. Everyday clothes in medium blue and camouflage green.

In case somebody had asked her how their love had developed, she would have remained silent. For persistently asking people she would have arranged the sentences in other contexts and would have exchanged the meaning of the words in a subtle way while defining them slightly different. However, but in sufficient way to give them another meaning, to let them create other associations in the head of the counterpart for being in a position to keep private, what has really happened.

Somebody played piano above the roofs of the narrow alley. He remained silent and beamed at her with joy. With gratitude they accepted the gift of love as it has made them happy in a profound way, as it comprises all facets of their being.

Die durchsichtige Leichtigkeit der Sensibilität

Nachdem die Vorbesprechung für eine offizielle Veranstaltung beendet war, wurde die Texterin Meriam von ihrem Kunden als Duettsängerin eingeladen. Es war ein Tag, an dem ihre berufliche Rolle es ihr erlaubte, sie selbst zu sein. Sie trug ihren alten, zotteligen schwarzen Lieblingspullover und hatte bereits mit der Band geprobt.

Auf die Wucht ihrer Begegnung war sie nicht vorbereitet. Sie hatte das Gefühl, Kinder von ihm bekommen zu wollen. Es war ihr Glück, dass ihre Begegnung fast verborgen vor der Welt stattfand. Die, die sie bemerkten, schwiegen.

Er war kein langsamer Mann. Seine Entscheidungen, die schnell und treffsicher zu sein schienen, hatte er im Vorhinein gründlich durchdacht.

Seine Kleidung war unauffällig, sie verriet seine Position nicht. Alltagskleidung im mittleren Blau und tarnfarbenen Grün.

Wenn sie jemand gefragt hätte, wie sich ihre Liebe entwickelt hatte, hätte sie geschwiegen. Bei hartnäckig Nachfragenden hätte sie die Sätze in andere Kontexte gesetzt und die Bedeutung der Wörter subtil ausgetauscht, indem sie sie geringfügig anders definierte. Jedoch genügend, um ihnen eine andere Bedeutung zu geben, im Kopf ihres Gegenübers eine andere Assoziation entstehen zu lassen, um das tatsächlich Geschehene für sich behalten zu können.

Über den Dächern der engen Gasse spielte jemand Klavier. Er schwieg und strahlte sie an. Sehr dankbar nahmen sie das Geschenk der Liebe an, die sie zutiefst glücklich machte, weil sie alle Facetten ihres Seins umfasste.

Die Sonne scheint immer

"When happiness returns
it burns my desire
to admire
the fire
of reality's complexity.
When happiness returns."

"When happiness returns
I will wear a yellow dress
with two white flashes of lightness
in the sun's yellow mightiness.
When happiness returns."

"Die Sonne scheint immer", liest die indische Tänzerin A'nah auf der Torüberschrift zu einem Glasgebäude.

Sie begrüßt ihre Freunde. „Ungeheuer schön!", sagt die in der Schweiz lebende Tänzerin Lia. „That's mighty nice!", bestätigt ihr schottischer Kollege Oscar. „¡Esto es espléndido!", ruft die spanische Tänzerin Liliana begeistert und die italienischen und französischen Tänzer Alessio und Adrien stimmen zeitgleich ein: „E'splendido!", „C'est splendide!"

„Ist es wahr? Scheint die Sonne immer?", fragt A'nah. Ihre Freunde lachen.

Riesige Seifenblasen, die eine junge Frau mit einem Seil
entstehen lässt, eiern sehr langsam durch die Luft. Ein
Musikapparat spielt einige Songs für sie. Kinder jagen
Ihnen nach, während die Sonne die Seifenblasen in allen
Farben leuchten lässt.

The sun is always shining

'When happiness returns
it burns my desire
to admire
the fire
of reality's complexity.
When happiness returns'.

'When happiness returns
I will wear a yellow dress
with two white flashes of lightness
in the sun's yellow mightiness.
When happiness returns'.

'The sun is always shining', A'nah, the Indian dancer reads
above the gate of the entrance to the glass building.

She welcomes her friends. 'Ungeheuer schön!', says the
dancer Lia who lives in Switzerland. 'That's mighty
nice!',her Scottish colleague Oscar confirms. '„¡Esto es

espléndido!', shouts the Spanish dancer Liliana enthusiastically and the Italian and the French dancer Alessio and Adrien join in simultaneously 'E'splendido!", „C'est splendide!'.

‚Is it true? Is the sun always shining?', asks A'nah. Her friends are laughing.

Hugh soap bubbles which a young woman creates with a rope wobble very slowly through the air. A music box plays some songs for them. Children chase after them while the sun lets the soap bubbles glow in all colours.

Sonnenchameleon

A'nah and her friends walk through the gate into a glass building which was built in the form of a sun chameleon. They meet the inventor Ariana. 'I asked people to build this building on the premises of my glass enterprise as it can be used for events very well', she explains to A'nah and her friends. 'The form is unusual', the Swiss notices. With Matthieu I got in contact some years ago with a green veiled chameleon which has sunny yellow strips on its flanks.

We found it fascinating and now it is always with us in this way', she explained to the amazed dance performance group. Moreover, it was in love with a rose stem, which was always expected by blossoming rose ladies in all colours. They quickly ran to him as soon as they saw him and embraced him. Well, sometimes he could manage it to get himself to safety', Ariana added with a smile. They go into the glass building.

'Some time ago we have invented a new procedure to create glass. A chameleon has nanocrystals made of guanine in its skin layer. The distance between each other differs in accordance to their mood and incidence of light. We have learned this mechanism. When an event is happening in this building with relaxed people, the chameleon glass is turning green. It creates a red colour when people are getting excited. We use this mood barometer to guide it into the desired direction. Language is the key to success. Glass as a seismograph which increases the chances of success to receive customer orders.'

The French dancer and physicist Adrien, who invests in innovative products, thinks that the mechanism is fascinating. He asks Ariana to explain it in detail later.

'Why is the glass building not called 'Sonnenchamäleon' (i.e. 'sun chameleon')? Liliana asks Ariana. 'The programmer is an Englishman who both lives in Madagascar, the land of chameleons and the Isle of Wight. He decided for the English variant of 'Chamäleon', Ariana added.

Sonnenchameleon

A'nah und ihre Freunde gehen durch das Tor in ein Glasgebäude, das in Form eines Sonnenchamäleons gebaut wurde. Sie treffen auf die Erfinderin Ariana. „Ich habe dieses Gebäude auf dem Gelände meines Glasunternehmens bauen lassen, weil es für Veranstaltungen sehr gut nutzbar ist", erklärt sie A'nah und ihren Freunden. „Die Form ist ungewöhnlich", bemerkt die Schweizerin. „Mit Matthieu habe ich vor einigen Jahren ein grünes Jemenchamäleon kennen gelernt, das sonnengelbe Streifen auf seinen Flanken hat. Wir fanden es faszinierend und es ist auf diese Weise immer bei uns", erklärt sie der verblüfften

Tanzartistengruppe. Es war übrigens in einen Rosenstengel verliebt, der immer von blühenden Rosendamen in allen Farben erwartet wurde. Sie liefen schnell zu ihm, sobald sie ihn sahen und umarmten in. Na ja, manchmal schafft er es auch, sich rechtzeitig in Sicherheit zu bringen", ergänzte Ariana lachend. Sie gehen in das Glasgebäude hinein.

„Vor einiger Zeit haben wir ein neues Glasherstellungsverfahren erfunden. Ein Chamäleon besitzt Nanokristalle aus Guanin in der Hautschicht, deren Abstand sich je nach Gemütszustand und Lichteinfall ändern. Wir haben uns diesen Mechanismus angeeignet. Wenn in diesem Gebäude eine Veranstaltung mit entspannten Menschen stattfindet, färbt sich das Chamäleonglas grün. Regen sich die Menschen auf, entsteht eine Rotfärbung. Wir nutzen dieses Stimmungsbarometer, um die Veranstaltung in die von uns gewünschte Richtung zu lenken. Sprache ist der Schlüssel zum Erfolg. Glas als Seismograph, der die Erfolgschancen erhöht, Kundenaufträge zu erhalten.

Der französische Tänzer und Physiker Adrien, der in innovative Produkte investiert, findet den Mechanismus faszinierend. Er bittet Ariana, ihn später im Detail zu erklären.

„Warum heißt das Glasgebäude nicht „Sonnenchamäleon"? fragt Liliana Ariana. „Der Programmierer ist ein Brite, der abwechselnd im Chamäleonland Madagaska und auf der Isle of Wight lebt.

Er entschied sich für die englische Variante von „Chamäleon", ergänzt Ariana.

Sonnige Zeiten

Im Chamäleonraum, der sich nebenan befindet, nimmt man zwar die äußeren Eigenschaften wie ein Chamäleon an", teilte Lia ihre Erfahrung mit. "Aber man bleibt trotzdem immer man selbst. Du kannst einen schwierigen Wettbewerber, der Dir persönlich nicht ähnlich ist, unter der Tarnkappe des Chamäleons unbeachtet beobachten. Du lernst auf eine fließende Weise seine Gedanken und Haltungen kennen und kannst auswählen, welche Du übernehmen möchtest, ohne dich mit ihnen identifizieren zu müssen. Zudem kannst Du sie nach dem Experiment wieder loslassen."

Wenn Du außerdem seine Verhaltensweisen und emotionale Färbung annimmst, wird er Dich nicht als Gegner ansehen. Das verschafft Dir Zeit für die optimale Strategie und schützt Dich gleichzeitig vor Übergriffen. Techniken, die man nur in der sonnigen Schönheit eines Experimentes einüben kann." „Dann könnte man diese Taktik auch nutzen, um jederzeit Urlaub zu haben, egal in welchem Umfeld man sich gerade befindet", überlegt Oscar und trinkt einen Schluck Wasser aus einem pastellgelben Glas. „Dazu müssen wir noch ausführliche

Experimente machen", grinst Liliana. „Das wären sonnige Zeiten!"

Sunny times

'In the chameleon room, which is next to this room, you are adopting the outer appearances like a chameleon', Lia shares her experience. 'However, you still remain yourself. You can watch a difficult competitor who is not similar to you under the magic hood of a chameleon. In this way you can get to know thoughts and behavior in a flowing way and you can choose which one you want to adopt without having to identify with them. Moreover, you can let them go after the experiment.

In addition, when you assume the competitor's behavior and emotional colouring he will not regard you as his enemy. This buys you time for the best strategy and protects you from attacks at the same time.
Techniques you can only practice in the sunny beauty of an experiment.' 'Then you could also use these tactics to have holidays at any time, no matter of the surrounding you are currently in', Oscar thinks and drinks a gulp of water from a pastel yellow glass. 'We have to make detailed experiments for it', Liliana grins. 'That would be sunny times!'

Historical trade beads

'The sun was so important for the Celts that they celebrated sun feasts', Ariana echoes Liliana's words. 'We have built the 'sun chameleon' here in Ghent as the town originally emerged from old Celtic settlements. Our potential customers shall experience glass and its purposes in the next month barefooted via smooth and less smooth glass surfaces, with different glass colours, glass thicknesses, wavy, warm and cold glass as well as with their intended purposes.

All this shall be embedded in your dance performances for which Meriam will write texts and set them to music, so that you can dance them. Celtic ritual dances are good as ice breakers. A'nah will practice some dances for amateurs with her husband, who is a former analyst.

Their daughter really wants to scatter historical trade breads and flowers around the sun. As already mentioned before our meeting, there will be a room called 'Wadi Natrun', 'Venice/Murano' at various places in Ghent, so that the history of glass will become clear in some exemplary, exquisite facets.

The episode 'Glasblowers' will be danced outside on a forest glade. I will let you know more about it – at the right time.' 'In the nick of time' says Oscar. 'En el momento preciso', laughs Liliana and Adrien adds with Alessio 'Au bon moment', 'Proprio al momento giusto'.

Historische Handelsperlen

„Die Sonne war so wichtig für die Kelten, dass sie Sonnenfeste feierten", nimmt Ariana Lilianas Worte auf. „Wir haben das „Sonnenchamäleon" hier in Gent gebaut, weil die Stadt ursprünglich aus alten keltischen Ansiedlungen entstanden ist. Unsere potentiellen Kunden sollen im nächsten Monat barfuß eine sinnliche Glaserfahrung mit glatten und weniger glatten Glasoberflächen, mit unterschiedlichen Glasfarben, Glasdicken, welligem, warmem und kaltem Glas sowie deren Verwendungszwecken machen.

All dies soll in Eure Tanzperformances eingebettet werden, für die Meriam die Texte schreiben und vertonen wird, damit ihr sie tanzen könnt. Keltische Kulttänze sind gut als Eisbrecher. A'nah wird mit ihrem Mann, einem ehemaligen Analysten, einige Tänze für Laien einüben.

Ihre Tochter möchte unbedingt historische Handelsperlen und Blumen um die Sonne herum verstreuen. Wie schon vor unserem Treffen erwähnt, gibt es an verschiedenen Orten in Gent einen Raum namens „Wadi Natrun", „Venedig/Murano", so dass die Geschichte des Glases in einigen exquisiten Facetten exemplarisch deutlich wird.

Die Episode „Glasbläser" wird draußen in einer Waldlichtung getanzt. Ich werde Euch mehr darüber erzählen – zur rechten Zeit." „In the nick of time", sagte Oscar. „En el momento preciso", lachte Liliana und Adrien

ergänzt mit Alessio „Au bon moment", „Proprio al
momento giusto."

Der Humor des Lebens

Der Humor des Lebens betritt die Sonnenterrasse seiner besten Freundin Meriam, der er den Spitznamen „Meritaton" gegeben hat, was „Geliebte des Sonnengottes Aton" bedeutet. Sie trinken griechischen Bergtee.

Meriam lebt glücklich im Paradies, lebt sie doch ausschließlich von den Aufträgen, die sie sich erträumt hat.

Sie hat gerade einen Anruf ihrer Freundin Ariana erhalten, die sie bittet, tanzbare Texte auf Deutsch und Englisch für verschiedene Glasminiaturperformances zu schreiben. Kein einfacher Auftrag, sollen einige Texte doch allgemein sein, damit man sie abwandeln und anpassen kann, während andere Texte spezielle Themen beinhalten sollen. Zudem sollen sie tanzbar sein und Textausschnitte ermöglichen. Anschließend soll sie sie auch noch vertonen. Meriam freut sich auf ihre neue Herausforderung. Sie lacht sie an und heißt sie willkommen.

Meriam liebt Partys mit Live-Musik, wo sie sich tänzerisch exzessiv und expressiv ausleben kann. Sie erinnert sich an eine durchtanzte Nacht. Der Nachklang des orgiastischen Gefühls erreicht sie und lässt ihre Hände tanzen.

Sie denkt daran, wie sie ihren Partner zum ersten Mal traf und wird sich der ungeheuren Dynamik und der poetischen Schönheit ihres Lebens bewusst. „Wenn die

Arbeit darin besteht zu träumen", zwinkert sie dem Humor des Lebens zu.

The Humour of Life

The Humour of Life enters the sun terrace of his best girlfriend Meriam, who he has given the nickname 'Meritaton', which means 'lover of the sun god Aten'. They drink Greak mountain tea.

Meriam happily lives in paradise as she exclusively lives from orders she has dreamed of.

She has just received a call of her girlfriend Ariana, who asks her to write danceable texts in German and English for various glass miniatures. No easy offer as some texts should be general ones, so that they can be modified and be adjusted, while other texts shall contain special topics. Moreover, they should be danceable and make text excerpts possible. Subsequently she shall set them to music. Meriam looks forward to her new challenge. She laughs at it and welcomes it.

Meriam loves parties with live music where she can act out her dancing in an excessive and expressive way. She thinks of a night of dancing. The echo of an orgiastic feeling reaches her and makes her hands dance.

She remembers the time she met her partner for the first time and becomes aware of the tremendous dynamic and the poetic beauty of her life. 'When the work consists in dreaming', she winks at the Humour of Life.

Sun light point

In order to dream you require a protected room. When
sitting in a sun light point you are protected from being
discovered by dazzling light particles.

'The sun is always shining'.

Do you agree to this content or do you prefer the content
of the poem?

'When happiness returns
it burns my desire
to admire
the fire
of reality's complexity.
When happiness returns.'

'When happiness returns
I will wear a yellow dress
with two white flashes of lightness
in the sun's yellow mightiness.
When happiness returns.'

The eyes are getting used to the prevailing light
conditions, but do they adopt to the psychological
condition, too?

Time to dream is time in which you do not embody a

professional or private role, but you stay in the various realms of beings for a shorter or longer period of time.

You can completely flop yourself into a world of thoughts or into a thought, get involved in a network of ideas, their fragments and ways of being which do not serve reality, but inspire it.

As they enable interactions which make visible what has been invisible before and enable the dreamer to float in feelings uninhibitedly. Integrated in an eternity of colourful pictures which can contain visions. Sometimes they work on the dreamer to realize them. Dreaming in a forum without an audience. Dreaming is grace, is talent, is gift.

Sonnenlichtpunkt

Zum Träumen braucht man einen geschützten Raum. Wenn man in einem Sonnenlichtpunkt sitzt, wird man von blendenden Lichtpartikeln vor dem Entdecktwerden geschützt.

"Die Sonne scheint immer".

Stimmt dieser Inhalt oder stimmen Sie eher dem Inhalt des Gedichtes zu?

"When happiness returns
it burns my desire
to admire
the fire
of reality's complexity.
When happiness returns."

"When happiness returns
I will wear a yellow dress
with two white flashes of lightness
in the sun's yellow mightiness.
When happiness returns."

Die Augen gewöhnen sich an die jeweiligen
Lichtverhältnisse, die seelische Befindlichkeit auch?

Zeit zum Träumen ist Zeit, in der man keine berufliche
oder private Rolle verkörpert, sondern sich in
verschiedenen Seinsbereichen kürzer oder länger aufhält.

Man kann sich komplett in eine Gefühlswelt oder einen
Gedanken fallen lassen, sich einbinden lassen in Geflechte
von Ideen, deren Fragmente und Daseinsformen gelangen,
die der Realität nicht dienen, sondern sie befeuert.

Weil sie Interaktionen ermöglichen, die vorher
Ungesehenes sichtbar machen und es erlauben in
Gefühlen zu schwelgen, ungehemmt. Eingebunden in eine
Ewigkeit von farbenprächtigen Bildern, die Visionen

enthalten können. Manchmal bearbeiten sie die träumende Person sie umzusetzen. Träumen in einem Forum ohne Publikum. Träumen ist Gnade, ist Gabe, ist Geschenk.

Zeit für Permanenz und Immanenz*

Es ist Zeit für Ariana, ein Gedankenexperiment zu machen. Sie geht in Ihren Ideengarten, wo sie Pflanzen zu vielen Themen züchtet. Sie setzt sich neben ihre Lieblingspflanze „Veränderung", die sich auch in ihrem Büro befindet. „Konzentriere Dich künftig mehr auf das Erfinden von Glasprodukten", flüstert sie ihr lächelnd zu. Ariana dankt ihr und die Pflanze versichert ihr, dass sie sie auch künftig beraten werde.

Ihr heutiges Gedankenexperiment bezieht sich auf globale Nomaden. Hochtalentierte Menschen, die zusammen die Firma verändern und wechseln, wie ein Freund von A'nahs Mann, der als Händler arbeitet. Sie haben nachfolgend in Düsseldorf sowie London in der gleichen Branche gearbeitet und sind jetzt in Zürich in Firmen unterschiedlicher Branchen angestellt. Ariana findet es faszinierend. Sie taucht tief in die Mentalität dieser Händler ein. „Sein und werden", denkt sie und identifiziert sich komplett mit ihnen. Sie erkennt, in welchen Grenzen die Händler denken und handeln und überschreitet sie nicht.

*Immanenz = Verbleiben in einem vorgegebenen Bereich (ohne Überschreitung der Grenzen)

Time for permanence and immanence

It is time for Ariana to make a thought experiment. She goes into her garden of ideas where she breeds plants for many topics. She sits next to her favourite plant 'change' which is in her office, too. 'Please concentrate more on inventing glass products in the future', it whispers to her with a smile. Ariana thanks it and the plant assures her that it will continue to advise her.

Her thought experiment today relates to global nomads. Highly talented people who change and leave the company together, like a friend of A'nah's husband who works as a trader. They have worked in Dusseldorf as well as in London and are now employed in different companies of the same sector in Zurich. Ariana finds it fascinating. She dives deep into the mentality of these traders. 'Being and becoming', she thinks and identifies herself with them completely. She recognizes the lines in which the traders think and trade and does not cross them.

*Immanence = staying in a defined range (without exceeding the limits)

smART

Meriam reads through the first drafts which she has
written this morning.

She crammes the notes into the beach bag and turns
herself on her smart, which Ariana has invented for an art
fair in New York. This is a thick, transparent glass plate
which works via solar cells. She says 'beach 'and her smart
drives her standing to the beach. The chirping of the
cicadas accompanies her like the keywords in her head.

Gorse and crowndaisies are expecting her there. Meriam
watches the opening blossoms while she is writing texts.
She finds out that the blossoms of two crowndaisies
require different lengths of time for opening. While she
can nearly watch one of the plants doing it, the other one
hardly needs a day for it.

smART

Meriam liest sich die ersten Entwürfe durch, die sie heute
Morgen geschrieben hat.

Meriam stopft die Notizen in die Badetasche und stellt sich
auf ihr smART, das Ariana für eine Kunstmesse in New
York erfunden hat. Dies ist eine dicke durchsichtige
Glasplatte, die mittels Solarzellen funktioniert. „Strand",
sagt sie und ihr smART fährt sie stehend zum Strand. Das

Zirpen der Zikaden begleitet sie wie die Stichworte in ihrem Kopf.

Ginster und Kronenwucherblumen erwarten sie dort. Meriam beobachtet die sich öffnenden Knospen, während sie die Texte schreibt. Sie findet heraus, dass die Blüten zweier Kronenwucherblumen unterschiedlich lange brauchen, um sich zu öffnen. Während sie bei der einen Pflanze fast dabei zusehen kann, benötigt die andere fast den ganzen Tag.

Das „O" der Schmetterlinge

Meriam schwimmt eine Runde im Meer.

Ein sehr gut durchtrainierter Mann mit nacktem
Oberkörper joggt an ihr vorbei, während ein weißer
Schmetterling auf der Kronwucherblume landet, die ihre
Knospen schnell öffnet.

Er erzählt Meriam vom „O" der Schmetterlinge. Meriam
hört interessiert zu. „Eigentlich gibt es zwei „Os", erklärt
ihr der Schmetterling. „Das „O" von „Humor ist ein Tor",
durch das wir oft fliegen. Dieses „O" nehmen wir aber nur,
wenn wir nicht durch unser Lieblings „O" fliegen können."

Zwei Zikaden biegen ein „O" aus der Kronwucherblume,
die ihre Blüten nur sehr langsam öffnet. Der Humor des
Lebens schlüpft hindurch. „Verrätst Du mir Eurer Lieblings
„O", bittet Meriam den Schmetterling. „Kennst Du den
Satz „Die Sonne scheint immer?", fragt er sie und der
Humor des Lebens ergänzt:

„Schmetterlinge fliegen durch das „O" des Wortes „Sonne"
wie durch ein Tor", sagt er. „Von der Sonne kommend
bringen die Schmetterlinge Wörter von gelben und weißen
Gegenständen mit, deren Repräsentanten sie sind."

The 'O' of the butterflies

Meriam goes for a swim in the ocean.

A well-conditioned man with his naked torso crosses her way while jogging as a white butterfly lands on the crowndaisy which opens her blossoms quickly.

He tells Meriam about the 'O' of the butterflies. Meriam listens with interest. Actually there are two 'Os' we often fly through. But we only take this 'O' when we cannot fly through our favourite 'O'.

Two cicadas curve an 'O' of the crowndaisy which opens her blossoms only very slowly. The Humor of Life slips through it. 'Will you tell me your favourite 'O', asks Meriam the butterfly. 'Do you know the sentence 'The sun is always shining?', he asks her and the Humor of Life adds:

Butterflies fly through the 'O' of the word 'Sonne' (i.e. 'sun') like through a gate', he says. 'Coming from the sun the butterflies bring along words of yellow and white objects whose representatives they are.

Meriam's notes

Many 1000 years old
Means of payment for the means of exchange silk, gold,
spices and as a status symbol
up to the 16th century Middle East, thereafter West Africa
investment, worn at initiation rites and weddings
colourfulness: blue – cobalt (not kobold☺), green-copper,
purple-manganese, yellow-iron, brown-iron oxide

Glassblowers
glass Germanic 'Glas', the gleaming, shining, amber
forest glassworks, a lot of wood for ovens cannot be
transported

Pigeon Egg Beads, transparent beads 1900-1950
Bohemia: wedding beads in drop shape or triangular form,
colourful, single-coloured, with lines, zebra stripes
Germany: bulled in glass tubes by hand, tiny diameter,
little Rocaille beads

Wadi Natrun
Wadi Natrun, Natrun Lake 100 km away from Alexandria
sodium bicarbonate for glass production
1450 before our time in Mesopotamia
sodium bicarbonate export
earliest glass production in the former Thebes, today
Luxor,
more than 1000 years before our computation of time

Venedig
Millefiori (1000 flowers) for more than 100 years from
Venice on the trade route to Africa
fear of fire of the glass ovens and town destruction,
fear that the art of beads generation was betrayed,
outsourced on the Isle of Murano in the year 1295
Chevron Beads, 1500 invited by the Venetians
12 point, star moulds in blue-white-red,
chrystallo, glass decolouration by manganese oxide
lattimo milk glass imitates Chinese porcelain

Meriams Notizen

Viele 1000 Jahre alt
Zahlungsmittel für die Tauschmittel Seide, Gold, Gewürze
und Statussymbol
bis zum 16. Jahrhundert Vorderer Orient, Mittelmeerraum
danach Westafrika
Wertanlage, getragen bei Initiationsriten und Hochzeiten
Farbigkeit: blau – Kobalt (nicht Kobold☺), grün-Kupfer,
violett-Mangan, gelb-Eisen, braun-Eisenoxid

Glasbläser
Glas germanisch „glaza", das Glänzende, Schimmernde,
Bernstein
Waldglashütten, viel Holz für Öfen sind nicht zu
transportieren
Pigeon Egg Beads, durchscheinende Perlen 1900-1950
Böhmen: Hochzeitsperlen in Tropfenform oder dreieckiger
Form, farbenfroh, einfarbig, mit Linien, Zebrastreifen
Deutschland: von Hand gezogene Glasröhrchen, winziger
Durchmesser, kleine Rocaille-Perlen

Wadi Natrun
Wadi Natrun, Natronsee 100 km von Alexandria,
Natronsalz für Glasherstellung
1450 vor unserer Zeitrechnung in Mesopotamien
Natronexport
Früheste Glasherstellung in früheren Theben, heute Luxor
mehr als 1000 Jahre vor unserer Zeitrechnung

Venedig

Millefiori (1000 Blumen) vor mehr als 100 Jahren von
Venedig auf dem Handelsweg nach Afrika

Angst vor Brand der Glasöfen und Stadtvernichtung,

Angst, dass Perlenerzeugungskunst verraten wird,

Auslagerung auf Insel Murano im Jahre 1295

Chevronperle, 1500 Venezianern erfunden

zwölfzackig, sternförmige Musterung blau-weiß-rot

chrystallo Glasentfärbung durch Manganoxid

lattimo Milchglas ahmt chinesisches Porzellan nach

Dolmetsch- und Übersetzungsdienst
Marion Wolters
Geprüfte Dolmetscherin Englisch

+++ Wirtschaft +++ Politik +++ Medien
+++ Energie +++ Literatur +++

Herstellung und Verlag: BoD- Books on Demand, Norderstedt
ISBN: 978-3-7481-5935-3